Deck the Paws

Spooky Cat #4

C.H. Lyn

Horizon Publishing

Contents

One

Silver ornaments hang from the rooftop of Nona's tall farmhouse. Strands of garland dip between them, the dark green at stark odds with how brown and gray everything is in the winter. The few evergreen trees on the property are decorated with tinsel and baubles–Kate's doing. A tradition from when she was a little girl and her family spent the holidays here.

I grin as Kate moves another outdoor ornament further up the tree. Missy watches it go, then gives me a squinty glare that would suggest it was *my* idea to make her new favorite pawing bag too high to reach.

Not that the increase of a foot will stop her. She'll be climbing the whole tree now.

It's cold. Not freezing like it will be in a few hours as the sun sets and the promised winter storm descends on us, but it is cold.

Skia huddles at the base of my neck, tucked into the black hood of my winter jacket. It's long, down past my knees, but my legs still feel the chill of the December afternoon air.

Nona strides out of the house with all the purpose and grace of an ancient woman with magic in her veins. Liz follows, a tray laden with odd magical components in her hands.

Liz has been an interesting addition to the farm. Her arrival, only a few weeks after a bounty hunter working for hell tried–and almost succeeded–to kill me, was the realization for the rest of us that the resurgence of magic in our world wasn't going to be slowing down anytime soon.

She'd pulled up in a taxi, which then promptly sped off. After walking up the drive and setting down her single duffle of personal items, she got straight to work helping a stunned Nona harvest her garden in preparation for the first frost.

As Nona put it, there's nothing wrong with an extra set of hands, and Liz has been a fixture at the farm ever since.

She appears to be in her mid-fifties, though her vocabulary fluctuates between an early-aughts teenager and someone who lived through 1920s high society, so it's practically impossible to tell how old she actually is. Neither Kate, Ags, or myself have had the courage to ask.

Given the map of wrinkles across her sunkissed skin, one thing we do know is how often she smiled, even before coming to the farm.

She's also very good, if as untrained as the rest of us, at magic.

"Come get what you need," Liz calls to Ags, who hurries over to survey the options.

Kate follows a moment later, and I wander over to look as well. I prefer to practice in private, but these weekend trips to the farm always include a group lesson of some sort.

That old anxiety of not knowing the answers to the test when everyone else has studied always creeps in when we do this. I'm not like the rest of our little magical group. Not like Kate and Nona, with the blood of Eastern European witches running in their veins. Or like Ags, carrying innate magic from her Hispanic ancestors in every step. Or like Liz, who announced after pulling the last of the carrots on the day she arrived that she'd come to learn magic from someone who "knows what they're doing."

I have nothing but good old B-positive in my veins. Magic has been a bit more difficult on my end.

The tray of items has a feather, which fits with the spell I've been trying to master, so I move my mug to one hand and snag it.

Kate positions herself a few dozen feet from one of the thick hay targets set up at the far side of the yard. Ags does the same beside her. I set down my scorching mug and get between the two of them, staring down my bale of hay with a nervous glare.

"Demi first," Nona says as she takes the tray from Liz.

I puff out a sigh.

Liz settles on Ags's other side, an encouraging smile on her lips as she meets my hazel eyes with her sky blue ones.

"Clear eyes," Nona calls. Her slippers crunch on the gravel as she walks over to stand beside me. "Full breaths. Let that cold air fill every inch of your lungs."

I follow her instructions, inhaling through my nose and letting the chilly air sting its way into my chest. Skia stirs at my neck, and I smile, imagining my demon friend attempting to fill their shadowy form like the rest of us.

"Piercing today," Nona says. She rubs her gloved hands together. "Call your element, and get whichever it is all the way through those stacks. Demi, show us what you've been working on."

I swallow, then do the work of filling my lungs again. I run the feather through my fingers a few times, pouring my concentration into the softness of the feathers, the pointed end of the shaft, and the memory of things like this falling through the air and catching the wind.

Warmth stirs within me. Heat that begins in my belly and grows to replace the cold air in my lungs. I tap my fingers together in a familiar pattern, swirling my hands to mimic the movement of the wind.

On my next exhale, I cast. A gust, frustratingly small, but a gust nonetheless, swirls toward the hay. The feather goes with it, the shaft barely reaching the center of the target before plunking against the packed hay and falling to the ground.

I straighten, forcing a smile while the others applaud.

"You're getting better, Demi." Nona nods with approval.

I accept the compliment with thanks, and give shallow nods to Kate and Ags as they pat my shoulder when I walk by to fetch my mug. I move to stand under the decorated tree, watching as I wait for my hot cocoa to get cool enough to sip.

"*You* are *getting better,*" Skia says, their voice soft enough that I figure they're only in my head. "*Magic isn't easy.*"

I shrug, watching Nona step up to Kate's side for a bit of instruction before her turn.

"*We should talk to Nona about finding you a focus.*"

I shrug again. It's been discussed, and I've tried a handful of the magical items Nona has at the farm. Nothing has helped amplify my spellcasting.

Skia's little voice in my head sighs. Then they say, *"It's cold, Demi."*

I pull my hood up, letting it sit loose on my head so they can be insulated on all sides. A low murmur of thanks follows. I blow on my hot cocoa and turn my attention away from my less-than-impressive showing to watch my friends.

Kate nods at Nona's final words, then gives me a "why me?" look behind her grandmother's back.

I chuckle silently, wrapping my fingers around my mug to warm them.

Kate faces her target with her feet planted firmly. Her fingers move, twisting a thin chord of twine into a series of complicated-looking knots. She pulls one hand to her chest, the other stretching toward the hay bale. At the moment the twine goes taut she murmurs something under her breath.

Ice forms along the twine, growing as it approaches her outstretched hand. In a split second it goes from thin crystals to a chunk of ice the size of her palm. It flies forward, slamming into the upper right corner of the hay and sending a burst of yellow strands flying.

"Yes," Ags shouts, giving Kate a wide smile.

I tap my hand against my mug. "That was bigger than last time, Kate. Nicely done."

She flashes me a grin, then turns to Nona.

"Well done," her grandmother says. "Sharper next time, and centered on the target. The sharpness will come from intent, and the center from focus."

Kate nods, her lips slipping into a thin line as she takes in Nona's words.

"Ags, Ags, Ags!" I call, like a spectator watching a game.

Ags plants her body sideways, like a pitcher facing home plate, palms pressed together at her chest as she glares down the target. "Okay," she murmurs. "Let's go."

She starts with a series of whispered words. I try to catch them but am distracted by a gentle tinkling sound.

I cock my head, listening. A familiar ringing of bells pulls my attention from the lesson, and I glance up just in time to watch Missy realize she's climbed too high on the tree. She looks down at me, her yellow eyes round with alarm. She yowls, swats her target–the ornament Kate just finished moving–and falls with it, both the silver bauble and the black cat tumbling down.

The bauble smashes on the ground. The cat lands in my arms.

My mug clatters across the gravel, cracking in two as my chocolatey goodness sinks into the not-yet-frozen ground.

Despite the commotion, Ags manages to hit her target, leaving a scorching hole in the center of the hay. She turns to laugh with the others as Missy looks up at me with all the repentance a cat can muster.

Which is to say, not much.

Two

"*W*hat do you think it'll be?" Skia asks, zipping around the apartment on Missy's back as the cat chases a tuft of lint.

I finish making the bed and come around the dividing wall to the sitting area. "I've got no clue. Agatha didn't give any details. She just said she thinks she found a focus for me with the new set of books she got in."

"*A book isn't a good focus.*" Skia leaps from Missy's back in a graceful arc, landing on the kitchen counter and looking up at me with their bright red eyes. "*It'll be too big.*"

"I doubt it's a book." I pick up my coffee mug and heave a sigh at the dregs remaining.

It's been a slow morning. Out the window, the tail end of a winter storm drops fat clumps of dry snow onto the city streets. Kate dropped us off right as the first flakes began to fall last night, and now there's nearly a foot of the stuff on the sidewalk below. We're supposed to get even more tonight.

I made the three of us eggs and jalapeno sausage, used up the last of my coffee beans, and watched the first half of the old Rudolph movie (Skia threatened to send the mean claymation reindeer to the third pit of hell before I calmed them down with a candy cane). It *was* going to be a quiet day at home.

Ags texted around 9am though, having made her way to the Emporium early to run through the new inventory. Inventory which included something for me. And, while there is the option to go over in a couple days after tonight's storm and when the snow melts, something in my gut tells me to tough out the cold and at least go check it out.

I look at Skia. "Wanna get hot chocolate on the way?"

They spin so fast they look like a tornado of shadow.

I pull the key bowl out of their way with a laugh. "That's a yes. Missy," I call. "Do you still want to come?"

My little cat freezes, her paws wrapped around the end of a strand of green garland I hung over the windows after we got home from Nona's last night. A weekend spent making cider, decorating, and planning for the winter solstice got me in more of a holiday mood than I've been in for quite a few years.

She retracts her claws, the garland going limp as she meets my squinting eyes. With fluid swiftness, she sits straight, lifting a paw and delicately licking it as though I didn't just catch her in the act.

I point at her. "If you mess up the decorations, I'm not putting them back up. You're a pretty kitty, Missy. You deserve some pretty holiday spirit. Don't mess it up."

Skia chuckles in my head, drifting from the counter as I pull on my jacket and settling into the oversized left pocket. *"Yes, Missy. I'll be very upset if you ruin my new hiding spot."*

Missy yowls and scampers over to wait while I lace up my snow boots.

"She's jealous, you know," Skia pokes their head out of the pocket. *"She's too heavy to sit up there on the garland, but it's perfect for me."*

I shake my head with a smile, pick up my cat, and carry the three of us downstairs and out into the cold winter air.

The coffee shop a block down the street is open. Only two patrons sit inside, each typing away on their computers. They look up as the bell above the door tinkles. I get a smile and nod from both, and return the gestures.

The barista behind the counter recognizes me and offers Missy a pet biscuit. I pay for a large hot chocolate (with plans to pour some into a bowl for Skia when we get to Agatha's). It only takes a minute for the drink to come out. A baggie with more treats for Missy sits beside it, and I tuck another two dollars into the tip jar before putting my wallet and the bag into my empty pocket, slipping my gloves back on, and stepping back into the snow.

The air is a special kind of cold. The kind that leaves an odd lack of scent. And freezes nose hairs. Missy huddles close on my shoulder.

The city has never been so quiet. Though the streets were plowed early, there aren't many cars risking the slick ground.

The insulating snow muffles footsteps, conversation, and all the usual noise of downtown.

We're only a block away from Agatha's Emporium when something smashes on the ground behind me. I whip around. A trash can halfway down the street lies dented in the snow.

I watch for a second, but nothing else moves.

"*Huh,*" Skia says. "*That was weird.*"

"Yeah," I murmur. I turn back around and take half a step when someone smacks into my right side.

My hot chocolate goes flying as I stumble back with an oomph. Missy yowls, claws digging into my jacket. A bundled figure hurries past with no apology.

I pull Missy into my arms, checking her first before turning to glare after the person. They move quickly, rounding a corner before I have a chance to shout that they need to watch where they're going.

I sigh. My breath comes out as a cloud of vapor. My hot chocolate stains the snow a rich brown color, and I grind my teeth.

"*That was almost as rude as those reindeer from earlier.*"

I nod. "Yeah. Okay. Hot chocolate *after* we see Ags. Let's go."

I pick up the cup and lid, tossing them in the trash as we continue on our way. With decidedly less excitement in my step I get us the rest of the way, kick the snow off my boots, and push open the door to Agatha's Emporium.

Three

Agatha's Emporium is decked out. Not for a traditional Christmas season, but for all things winter solstice. There are garlands of ivy, evergreen bows, and other various greenery strung along every wall. Candles (the battery powered kind for safety) sit among the trinkets and books. Signs with a variety of seasonal sayings brighten the darker corners of the shop.

The bell above the door tinkles as we step in. I shut the door as Missy leaps from my shoulder and winds her way through the shelves to greet Ags at the back.

"Heyya cutie," Ags says, petting Missy with long strokes along her back.

"*Heyya back,*" Skia hisses, humor in their tone. "*I see you've successfully avoided the perils of your icy planet.*"

Ags snorts. "Icy planet, huh? We should take you up north next winter."

I chuckle. "Christmas in Winnipeg sounds terrifying."

Skia hurrumphs.

The countertop is crowded with things. Missy steps gingerly over a crumpled ball of packing paper and sniffs at a tall pile of books.

"You got a new shipment?" I ask, unnecessarily.

A quick scan of the stacks of books don't show anything that could be a focus. Part of me doesn't want to seem too eager. Another part of me knows how silly that is. Ags and I are close. She knows how much I want to be better at magic.

"Yeah." Ags swipes the packing paper onto the floor behind the counter. With a grunt, she lifts one stack of books and moves them aside. "A lot of this is for customers. Just some fun wiccan stuff, notebooks, the usual."

I nod, lifting a wrapped bundle of leafy-covered notebooks and moving it to join the books for the shop.

"*Anything* else?" Skia asks with emphasis.

I grimace.

Ags grins. "As a matter of fact..." She shifts another few books–these much older with broken spines and delicate covers–and pulls a small green velvet bag to the front.

A thrill of excitement–or nerves–runs down my spine. I exhale as she pulls the silver strings loose.

The bell above the door tinkles.

Ags meets my eye for a sec, then swipes the bag down beside the cash register and hurries around the counter. "Hello," she calls in a cheerful voice.

My gaze goes from the spot where the bag disappeared, to the stack of magical tomes still on the counter. Books we definitely *don't* want someone to see and try to buy.

I heft the stack, walk through the curtain behind the counter, and deposit them on a crate in the back.

"*Demi*," Skia's frantic voice calls. "*You'd better get out here.*"

I frown and rush back into the main section of the store.

I am greeted by pandemonium. Ags is in the middle of the store, bracing a half-tipped shelf while trying to stop a collection of crystal glasses from cascading to the ground. Missy yowls loudly, sprinting through the store after... are those kittens?

Skia is nowhere to be seen, though I assume that's on purpose because a young person with wild hair and frantic eyes is also running through the store after the cats.

"What the–" A split second of hesitation freezes me, then I hurry to Agatha's side and help her straighten the shelf.

She darts away the moment it's righted, rushing after the still scurrying felines.

"I'm so sorry," the person–a young woman, I think–calls from where she's crouched behind the counter. She stands up, a kitten in each arm. The little creatures are pawing at each other and hissing.

Missy hops onto the countertop and stares at them with a shrewd, disapproving expression. I catch sight of an unnatural shadow beneath the cushy chair in the corner. At least Skia managed to avoid the commotion.

"Are you all right?" Agatha demands. She seems to realize her tone and takes a deep breath.

From the clothes alone, it's clear this woman is unhoused. Maybe couch surfing, or living out of her car. She's well layered, but every article has stains or holes or both. Her hands are dry, the skin chapped and ungloved. She's in a rough spot–especially with this weather.

I give Ags a chance to settle her features by stepping forward and addressing the woman. "I'm Demi, this is Agatha. Welcome to the Emporium. Are the kittens okay? Are you okay?"

The woman's wide gaze takes me in; the question there is one I'm used to. After a second, she nods. "I'm sorry again. They got away from me. They're still little and don't listen all that well."

"It's okay." I gesture to the mostly-unharmed interior of Agatha's shop. "No harm done. Were you looking for something specific? Or just getting out of the snow?"

"Oh." She stammers over her words, stepping out from behind the counter and moving toward the front. "I was just... checking it out. I like books and um..." She looks around. "Candles."

I turn with her, following as she backs up to the door. My eyebrow raises, suspicion beginning to outweigh sympathy.

"I'll get out," she says. "Didn't mean to cause a fuss."

"Hang–" Ags calls from behind me, but before she finishes speaking, the woman has shoved open the door and darted back into the cold.

The store is quiet for a few long seconds. I watch as the woman disappears from sight, pushing her way through the growing snow.

Ags comes to my side, hands on her hips and a frown on her face. "Well. That was odd."

"Yeah," I mutter. "I wish she hadn't left so quick. We could have offered her some food or something."

"*I think she'll be fine,*" Skia hisses. They float along the ground, coming up and settling onto a nearby shelf.

"What makes you say that?" Ags asks, turning back to the store and straightening some of the off-kilter items.

"She took plenty of money from the register before she left."

I freeze. Ags does the same. Simultaneously, we turn to stare at Skia.

"I take it that's not a good and normal thing for humans to do..." they say slowly.

Dread digs into my chest.

Ags grits her teeth and squeezes her eyes closed for a second. "What?!"

Four

Both of us scramble toward the check-out counter. Skia's right. The cash register is open, only a few crinkled ones and the coins remain.

The tray itself is cracked. It looks like something was used to break it open.

I press my fingers to my forehead, frustration chasing away any holiday spirit brought on by the snow. "What the hell. That's awful. I'm sorry, Ags."

She turns to me, tears welling in a way that magnifies her beautiful brown eyes. "It's not the cash I'm worried about, Demi."

I frown, head cocking to the side.

She sniffs and gestures to the empty register. "That's where I put the focus."

It takes a second for it to click. Then my shoulders droop. Sound seems far away as her words shatter the hope and excitement I'd been foolishly holding onto. I puff out a sigh, my chest heavy and tight.

"It's okay." I shake my head. "We didn't know if it was going to work anyway."

Ags puts a hand on my arm. "I'm really sorry, Demi. Maybe we can track her down?"

"*I'd be happy to help you find the scoundrel.*" Skia hops lightly onto the counter, their red eyes glinting with anger. "*The disrespect.*" They give a little shake. "*I remember when people knew the price of stealing from witches.*"

A small smile breaks Ags's melancholy expression. "The snow is thick out there. But..."

She trails off, and I look up sharply. Ags stares at the unsorted books on the counter.

"Oh no," I mutter. "What now?"

She thumbs down the spines, then whirls and disappears into the back room.

"*I'm serious, Demi,*" Skia says. "*I'm a very skilled tracker.*"

I nod, my throat constricted. The bright energy of the morning feels as though it's been completely drained from me.

Missy rubs against my ankles. I tell her she's a good cat.

I pick up a few more things that were knocked down during the commotion and place them back in their spots on the shelf. It's a clever tactic. Using kittens to cause a distraction. I scratch behind Missy's ears.

Agatha comes out of the back room, tears drawing thick lines down her cheeks. "She took one of the books for Nona." She sniffs and tugs a tissue from a box on the counter. "The best one I found. It was really expensive and..." She twists her lips to the side, trying to keep her tears at bay. "It had the most information. Seemed the most legit."

I take a breath, meet Skia's eye, and nod again. "Okay. Let's go."

I turn on my heel, scooping my jacket from where I'd draped it over a chair when we came in. Any hesitation about going after the woman is gone with the presence of Agatha's tears. The money is frustrating, but it's early in the day and there wasn't much there. The magic focus was more. A deeper cut that hurt despite having not even seen the thing yet.

But making Agatha cry?

Skia hurries alongside me, leaping to my arm and then slithering into my pocket as I pull the coat on.

"Demi?" Ags follows us. "It's fine, really. It's too cold to–"

I face her for a second, looking up at my friend. The one by my side through a global pandemic. Through the following year of depression. The one who didn't blink an eye when she found out I'd adopted a demon. The one who helped me rescue said demon from awful, dangerous people. The one who quite literally saved my life.

"Can you watch Missy?"

The determination must come through in my face, because she gapes for a moment, and then nods.

"We'll be back."

Skia and I push through the door. The road is collecting a fine layer of snow. On the sidewalk, not even the salt is enough to stop icy patches from forming as the temperature drops once again.

"We may need to find her for more than getting that book back," Skia says, their voice uneasy as they sink deeper into my left pocket.

I puff out a breath, pulling gloves onto my hands and starting off.

The tracks aren't hard to follow. A trail of hurried footsteps, dragging pieces of cloth, and the occasional stumble from moving too fast is carved into the snow.

"I wonder if she was out here last night," I murmur, my voice muffled by the collar of my jacket. I've got it pulled up to my nose.

Skia doesn't respond, but I know they're wondering the same thing.

The streets are somehow emptier than they were before. The forecast called for another dump of snow, but not until evening.

It appears to be early.

We walk a full three blocks before the tracks end. Around a sharp corner, we're greeted by the entrance to a multi-level parking garage. Snow is scattered across the concrete, melting footsteps leading the way in.

"You ready?" I ask.

"Yep." Skia shifts in my pocket. *"Be careful, Demi."*

I step into the dark, frigid parking garage.

Five

Our footsteps are frustratingly loud in the vast echo chamber that is a parking garage. Despite the weather, we do pass a handful of people moving to or away from their cars. The tracks are gone, melted away by the concrete. Even if we could follow a water trail, there's been too much movement to discern what came from our thief and what came from a businessman in a trenchcoat.

"Any ideas?" I murmur. We've scoured the bottom floor with no luck. The stairwell takes us up to the next, but I'm worried we made a mistake staying here. Maybe she darted in and then back out.

"*She's still here.*" Skia pokes out of my pocket, looking up the stairs.

"Is that something you know from some demon sense? Or are you guessing?"

"I won't dignify that with a response," Skia scoffs. *"Keep going, Demi."*

I sigh and take the stairs past the second floor entrance and up to the third and final. The rooftop section is closed for the winter, so this is as far as we can go. The open air of this place, with slitted gaps in the concrete walls and the winding pavement leading back down, is lovely in the summer. Right now my teeth are chattering, and I wish I was wearing a fourth layer.

There are fewer cars up here. We circle the perimeter, and I halt abruptly as I come around a big SUV and catch sight of the far corner of the space.

A bundle of clothes and blankets is nestled into the corner. On it sits the woman who stole Agatha's book. I crouch down, immediately unsure how to do this. Sneaking up is creepy. Walking up gives ample time for her to run off again, though all of her things are here. Maybe she wouldn't run off. Maybe she'd leave the book.

"What is she doing?" Skia says in my head. They've crawled out of my pocket and now sit next to me, disguised as one of the many shadows criss-crossing through the building.

I peer around the side of the vehicle. The garage is dark, but there, in the mess of blankets I can see her hands. They're moving quickly. Twisting and bending and... sparking? Definitely sparking. I squint, watching as the sparks that seem to stem from her fingertips grow.

My eyes go wide as a small burst of flame appears in her palms. She exhales from the side of her mouth, clearly being careful not to breathe on the fire. The flame sits, hovering just above her amber skin.

She stares at it, brow furrowed. And then, maybe six or seven seconds after its appearance, it goes out. A frustrated "*Damnit*" echoes through the garage.

There is a soft meow. The kittens make an appearance from underneath the blankets. The two of them, an orange tabby and a white one with big black spots, pad toward her and nestle against her hands.

"You can do magic." My voice, as softly as I speak, carries.

I stand, the presence of magic negating my desire to be sneaky. Now I need more than Agatha's book back. I need answers.

The young woman looks up, her eyes wide as a doe's.

I put my hands up. "Please don't take off again. I came here to talk to you. And now…" I shake my head in disbelief. "Now I *really* need to talk to you."

She swallows, still frozen and watching me with wary eyes. "I don't want to talk. I don't have your money anymore. I can't give it back."

My stomach clenches with disappointment, but I shove it down. "That's fine," I say. "I'm not worried about any of that right now. You can do *magic*. I know a bit about that. I can help you."

Her eyes narrow at my last sentence. "I didn't ask for help."

I take another step forward, hands still raised. "I know. And if you don't want it, that's fine. But at least let me ask you a few questions, please. You're only like, the fifth person I know who can do magic like that."

The distrust in her gaze melts into curiosity, glimmers of excitement piercing through the concern. She looks down at her kittens. The two of them climb into her lap, each looking at each other and then her.

She returns her gaze to me. "Fine. We can talk for a minute. But only if you promise to keep that thing in your jacket."

Six

S kia tilts their shadowy form up to look at me. I raise my eyebrows and hold open my left pocket. They inflate and deflate, like a sigh. With a hurumph, they slip back into my pocket.

"How'd you know about Skia?" I ask, taking another few steps towards the woman.

"The cats," she says, as though that answers the question. "Don't get too close."

I nod, coming to a stop a couple of feet away from the edge of her bottom blanket. I sit down, criss crossing my legs and draping my jacket around my knees.

"I'm Demi." I fidget with the thin leather bands of my bracelet. "And the thing in my pocket is Skia. They're a sneeze demon."

"A nice sneeze demon," Skia mutters in my head. *"I don't want to scare her more, Demi. You let me know when I can properly introduce myself."*

I pat my pocket reassuringly.

The woman blinks. Her hands shift to scratch behind the ears of the kittens. She takes a few seconds to digest my words, then gives a shallow nod. "I'm Cynthia. This is Prince," she gestures to the orange cat, "and Princess." She pats the spotted one on the head.

"And they told you about Skia?"

Cynthia shrugs. "They tell me a lot of things. But it's not always clear what they're talking about."

I nod. "It feels that way with Missy, my cat, sometimes. She's super smart, but it's hard to know what she's trying to tell me."

Cynthia snorts. I tilt my head.

She shakes her head. "No, I mean I can literally speak to them. It takes a lot of concentration, but if I listen just right I can hear what they're saying."

"Oh my."

"The actual cats..." I glance at the kittens. Their expressions are as cat-like as I've ever seen. Reminiscent of the way Missy used to be before a short possession by Skia. Now her eyes gleam with an intelligence far beyond a normal animal.

Cynthia nods. "The cats. They're very child-like the way they speak. Most animals are."

My eyes are so wide the cold is drying them out. I blink, the shock in my system like electricity buzzing through my veins.

None of us can do this. Not Nona, not Kate, not Liz, and not Ags. And certainly not me. Skia sometimes seems like they talk to animals, but I haven't figured out yet if that is them actually communicating with the pigeons we see on the street or if they're being their usual sarcastic and silly self.

Cynthia continues, her voice breathy and excited. I get the feeling that I'm the first person she's told all of this to.

"They don't have a strong sense of self, ya know? Older cats do, but even then it's not like how humans think about themselves. Cats are pretty one-track focused."

"How long have you had..." I want to ask how long she's had this ability, but I change the question mid-way. "Prince and Princess? They're very attached to you."

"*Attached?*" Skia says in my head. "*Hell, they helped her rob us.*"

She grins, and the smile gives heartbreaking insight into just how young she is. The clothes and hygiene make her appear much older.

"Since I aged out," she says with a shrug. "They were from a couple litters my last foster-family was trying to sell. When I packed up my stuff these two snuck into my bag." Cynthia chuckles, picking up Princess and snuggling the kitten close to her face. "They didn't want me to leave without them, huh sweetie?"

The kitten meows.

"*Demi... I didn't understand most of that. What is she talking about?*"

I do quick math. The cats are barely a few months old. Cynthia is *much* younger than I'd originally thought. Eighteen, and barely eighteen. If the kittens were old enough to leave their mom when she packed up, it's only been a month or two since she left foster care.

An old statistic cracks my heart a little more. Something like thirty percent of the kids who age out of foster care end up homeless in the years after they turn eighteen. The memory of my homelife at that time–of how much I wanted to be gone and how close I was to just running away–hits me hard.

I swallow and look at my hands. The soft weight of Skia in my pocket, the witch and cat waiting for me in a warm shop, the family of magical people expecting us for a solstice party in a few days, the magic–limited as it is–that I can create with only will and determination and focus...

In the face of this kid with her kittens, I count the blessings I'm lucky enough to have.

Then I take a deep breath and meet Cynthia's eye. "I want to introduce you to Skia. I promise, they're nice."

"*Very nice. Not at all like those nasty reindeer from that movie.*"

Given the way Cynthia jumps, it's clear Skia has spoken in both our heads.

I sigh with a smile. "Okay if I take them out?"

She hesitates, then nods.

"Come on out, Skia."

My demon friend slithers out of my pocket and settles on my lap, much like a cat would. They look up at Cynthia with glowing red eyes and a hard to read expression that *I* know is a smile.

"*Pleased to meet you, despite all the thievery earlier. You're clearly a very powerful witch. I look forward to seeing your magic in action.*"

Cynthia's jaw drops. A few seconds go by, and then she recovers and shakes her head. "Here I thought talking to cats was as weird as it got."

"It's a new weird for me," I say with a shrug. "None of my friends can do it."

She blushes. "It's come in handy a few times. I'm sorry to use it stealing from you. I was in a... bind. Owed someone. Unexpectedly."

I shrug again. The disappointment of losing what might have been a focus to help my magic has dulled. There are more important things now. "I'm not as worried about the money, but do you still have the book you took?"

Her cheeks go even darker, the flush reaching the roots of her hair. She pulls aside a blanket fold and reveals a thick leather-bound tome. She passes it over without a word.

I take it with an exhale of relief.

"*No chance of getting the rest of it back?*" Skia asks in a wry tone.

"Skia," I say, somewhat scoldingly.

Cynthia shakes her head, her eyebrows drawn together in a worried frown. "I already dropped it off. I'm sorry."

I shake my head. "Don't worry about it. Tell you what, to pay me back, why don't you come with us and talk to Ags. She's the one who owns the shop." I chuckle. "And as soon as she finds out you can do magic she's going to completely forget the money thing. We have a little group of people learning."

"Learning... magic?" Her tone is tinged with awe.

I smile. "Yeah. You'd be welcome. If you're interested. And we can just meet with Ags for now if you want."

Cynthia glances at the demon in my lap, then at the kittens in hers. "Can I bring Prince and Princess?"

My response is cut off by Skia. "*Do you think they'd do well on a farm?*"

Cynthia raises an eyebrow at me.

I laugh, shifting so I can get to my feet. "Let's worry about the farm later. Yes, they can come with us."

I dust off my butt; the cold of the concrete seeped through my pants and my legs are practically frozen. "Is there anything else you want to bring?"

She takes a minute packing up an old backpack with the few things she wants to bring with us. I have her stick the book in there too, as my jacket pockets do have a size limit. She pulls two of the thickest blankets around her shoulders. "I'll leave the rest." Her gaze meets mine, hope blazing in the dark depths of her chocolate-colored eyes.

We walk away from her corner in the parking garage, trundling down the stairs with Skia in my pocket and a pair of kittens in Cynthia's arms.

"You're sure what I'm doing is magic?" Cynthia asks when we reach the bottom. "I'm not like... cursed or something?"

I purse my lips for a second. Then I give her a "who knows" shrug. "If it's magic, my friends can help you learn to use it. If it's a curse... we can probably deal with that, too."

She pauses, then lets out a disbelieving laugh. "This is all–"

"*Weird,*" Skia says. "*We know. It's kind of our brand.*"

Seven

We move at a somewhat relaxed pace through the snow. The cold presses in on every side, but the let down of adrenaline from the previous hour has me lacking in urgency.

Cynthia walks half a step behind me, her gaze fixed on my pocket as she and Skia chat. Skia is telling her all about Nona's farm and giving her a rundown of everyone in our little magical family.

The grin on her face still has traces of disbelief, but the excitement is growing.

I step on a packed chunk of snow and slip. Cynthia catches my arm, helping me straighten up. I grimace.

"Let's stop for a few minutes and get some hot chocolate or something before we get back to Agatha. I need to warm up."

Cynthia's face reddens, but that might be the swift breeze of frigid air that hits us.

We head into the same coffee shop I stopped at barely an hour ago. The barista gives a smile and makes a joke about me being back already.

"What do you want?" I ask Cynthia as I stick my hand into my right pocket, fishing for my wallet.

I hesitate.

There's nothing in my pocket.

Cynthia winces, an apologetic smile tight on her face. "I... I'm sorry."

My jaw drops as Skia hisses in my head. "You're the one who ran into us this morning?"

She nods, then pulls her backpack around and fishes in a side pocket for a second. My wallet appears in her hand.

I snatch it from her, part of me annoyed, but mostly chagrined at my own lack of awareness for not noticing it was missing this whole time. I open it, stepping up to the counter to pay for three peppermint hot chocolates. After my card goes through and we move to the far end of the counter, I give Cynthia a squinty glare.

"I had a twenty in here."

She shrugs and says with a dry tone, "Yeah, that's why I had to find a place to get more cash."

My eyebrows come together in a bemused frown.

"*You said you owed someone?*" Skia asks.

Cynthia sighs. "Pretty much."

I'm close to asking what that means, but I don't want to pry too much too early. "You're all settled though?"

"Definitely." She nods with a firm set to her lips.

"Good enough for me," I say, pulling my phone out of an *inside* pocket of my coat.

"*You should keep your wallet in there too,*" Skia suggests.

"Agreed," Cynthia says, watching me. "It'll be harder to snatch."

"Thanks, you guys." My words come through gritted teeth, but with the return of Agatha's book and the excitement about finding a new magic user, I can't muster up any actual anger.

I shoot a quick text to Agatha letting her know the important bits. We've got the book, Cynthia can do magic, we're bringing her with us, and I'm getting everyone hot cocoa. She sends a laughing emoji at the last part.

We collect our hot chocolates and head back into the cold. The brief respite is enough for me to confidently pick up the pace to get us to Agatha's store. We turn down the final alley.

Cynthia sucks in a breath.

I glance at her, then follow her gaze.

A man in an expensive, thick winter jacket and matching gloves stands at the end of the alley.

Eight

"Hey, Cynthia," the man calls. His voice would echo, but the snow dampens the sound. He wears a wool cap, bits of sandy brown hair peeking out from the bottom. He's right in the middle of the alley, fully blocking our way.

Clusters of thick white snow collect on every surface around us. The storm isn't getting worse, but it hasn't moved on yet either.

"*It's always something,*" Skia sighs with the tone of an introvert well past their social battery drain. "*Who is this?*"

"Remember how I said I owed someone?" Cynthia murmurs.

"Yeah..." I grimace, glancing at the large hot chocolates I'm carrying in each hand. "I also remember you said you were settled."

"I am," she snarls. "I left him the money and a note." She raises her voice. "We're done, Fitz. I paid you for your help. That's it."

The man—Fitz—holds up a crinkled brown paper bag. "This? No, I don't think so." He walks forward at an annoyingly slow pace. Like he's trying for a bad-guy strut from a 90s movie. "I let you spend the night in my BMW. That's worth more than a hundred bucks and the random garbage in here."

My face scrunches in an expression of incredulity for a second. Then I turn to Cynthia. "You stayed the night in this guy's car?"

She nods. "Last night. He saw me in the parking garage and offered his apartment. *That* wasn't going to happen—"

"*Smart girl,*" Skia interrupts.

"But it was really cold, and I couldn't get the fire to..." She looks down at the folds of her draped blankets where the kittens are hiding. "This morning he said I owed him."

I exhale and turn to Fitz, gesturing with my hot chocolates. "Hey, man. She paid you more than a night in a motel is worth. That's enough. Take the win and walk away."

He scoffs, about fifteen feet away now. With a snide sneer he says, "Don't make this your business. She and I had a deal." He turns his attention back to Cynthia. "Listen, this doesn't have to be hard. Come with me; we'll go back to my place and sort it all out. I'd hate to get the cops involved."

A feeling, dark and burning like tar, crawls up my spine.

Cynthia blanches. "You... you said it was okay if I stayed in your car. I didn't break anything."

The fear and anxiety in her voice brings that dark feeling from my spine to my veins, pumping through my body like a toxin.

He shrugs and tosses the paper bag onto the ground. "Your choice. You'll pay up... one way or another."

And there it is. The grin that sends my anger spiraling into my chest, my lungs, my core. We've been dealing with supernatural assholes for the last year, and I'd almost forgotten how many mundane ones still exist in the world.

"*What does he mean?*" Skia asks.

"Nothing good," I mutter, my voice too low for Fitz to hear.

"Come on, Cynthia," Fitz calls, annoyance flaring in his tone. "I don't want you to spend the night in a jail cell, and you don't want that either. They won't let you keep those flea-bags. I'm offering you a warm place to stay. You should be grateful."

I release a tense breath. "Get in my hood, Skia."

The little demon does what I say, snaking up the back of my jacket and tucking into the oversized, baggy hood. I toss the hot chocolates a few feet away. Warm cocoa splashes onto the snow, the ruined cups melting their way to the ground.

"Grateful?" Cynthia demands, indignance breaking through the fear. "Are you serious?"

Fitz pulls out his phone. "Fine. Be that way. Cops'll find your prints all over my car. Last chance."

Nine

"*Are you thinking what I'm thinking?*" Skia asks as I pull the hood up over my head.

"I hope so," I murmur.

Fitz doesn't even look at me as I take a step forward. My fingers bend and twist, forming shapes and moving quickly. I reach within, feeling for the anger, pulling it forward, bringing it to my hands.

The wind picks up. Swirling flurries of snow no longer fall from the sky, they swirl around us.

"Back up," I say to Cynthia. My voice is low.

She does so, quickly. Ahead of us, Fitz has finally stopped looking at his phone.

I tilt my head forward, letting the hood fall even lower. Skia shifts, putting their shadowy form in front of my face.

"What..." Fitz's weak voice shakes.

I smile. My fingers work even faster, and the speed of the wind increases. A storm of snow builds, circling me and Skia as we step closer to the man.

My vision is hampered by the demon in my hood, but I can imagine the picture we make. A hooded form with smoke and glowing red eyes. Add in the magic...

A large cluster of snow hits Fitz's arm. I step forward again. The swirling tornado of ice around me is becoming dangerous now, and I hope Cynthia is far enough back.

"What is this?" Fitz demands, fear flickering across his eyes.

I've never done it like this before, wide and less controlled. It's always been narrowed in with a specific purpose. I suppose there is a purpose now. To terrify this man into leaving Cynthia alone for good.

He doesn't need to be hurt. But part of that will depend on if he's smart enough to back up.

I take another step.

The snow and ice strikes at his coat, his arms, his face. He raises a hand to block the wind. His phone melts the ice that sticks to it for a moment, but soon there is too much and the screen is covered in white.

"What's wrong with you?" Fitz chokes out. He's barely able to speak against the fury of the wind.

"*Me?*" Skia hisses, their voice loud in my head and likely even louder in his. The sweet tone they've adopted is gone. Replaced with a deep, demonic sound that reminds me of a different, much larger demon we faced together so long ago.

That splash of fear amplifies in Fitz's wide eyes.

"*I'm the terror in the night.*"

I don't step any further. The tight funnel of wind around me is just where I want it to be. Slamming Fitz in the face with snow.

"*The shadows in the storm. The* thing *that will come for you if you try to take advantage of someone like Cynthia ever again.*"

A chip of ice slices across his cheek, and a drop of blood oozes down his pale skin.

That seems to be enough for him.

Fitz yelps, hand going to his face as he stumbles backward. "Get away from me, you freak," he screeches. He trips, sprawling backwards into the snow.

I don't advance. The magic coursing through my arms feels red-hot. I'm reaching a breaking point. This is one of the things Nona has warned of, but I never thought I'd experience it myself.

In my head, Skia cackles with laughter. "*Run, whelp. Run and never forget this moment. If you do... I will return.*"

Fitz scrambles back several feet before flipping around onto all fours. He pulls himself to his feet and runs, slipping and sliding as he scurries away around the corner and off to wherever he came from.

I wait another second, my hands still moving with purpose. And then, when I'm sure he's gone, I drop my arms.

The winds die, snow and ice falls, silent, to the ground.

I fold in half, hands going to my knees barely in time to keep me standing. Skia falls out of my hood with an oomph, landing in the snow. I draw in deep breaths.

"Demi!" Cynthia's frantic voice comes to me through the thundering of my own heartbeat in my ears. She hurries to my side, a hand going on my arm as she bends down to look at me. "Are you okay? That was... I mean... thank you."

"*We are quite the team,*" Skia says, shimmying the snow off their smoky body. Their voice is back to normal. "*Now, someone put me in a pocket before I freeze.*"

I huff a chuckle and open the pocket of my jacket. Skia returns to their spot, sinking low into the fabric with a gentle hum.

"Thank you both." Cynthia helps me straighten up, holding my arm as a moment of dizziness causes me to sway.

"Happy to help," I groan. My stomach roils. I hold up a hand, dart to the side of the alley, and vomit. With one eye half-closed and my head pounding, I stand straight again, wincing. "I think I maybe overdid it a bit."

"*That was gross, Demi. And yes, yes you did. All for the better, I say. Besides, can you imagine Agatha's face when we tell her what we did!*"

They continue on, chattering away in my and Cynthia's heads as the two of us share a smile. Cynthia drapes my arm over her shoulder. The kittens leap from her coats, jumping around in the snow as we make our way out of the alley.

"Ohh," Cynthia mutters.

I follow her gaze. Princess has stopped at the side of the alley. The little spotted cat turns her head back to look at us, a brown paper bag in her mouth.

Laughter bubbles up from my stomach, and I make the pounding in my head even worse by letting it out. But I don't care.

Ten

We trudge into Agatha's Emporium, and I'm immediately assaulted by the furious yowling of a cat feeling left out of adventure.

Missy's tail narrowly avoids some of the more fragile items on the bookshelves as she deftly advances.

I crouch down, wincing at the way my neck hurts almost as much as my head now. "Hey girl. Sorry. I didn't want you out there in the snow, ya know?"

"That's not why she's mad." Cynthia hesitates in the doorway, letting gusts of cold sweep into the store. "She doesn't get why you brought me back with you."

I cup Missy's furry face. "She's a friend now, Missy. Someone Nona will want to meet."

Missy squints up at Cynthia for a second, then turns and flounces away.

I chuckle. "I think that's about as good as you're gonna get for now."

"Come in already," Ags says, hurrying to join us and gesturing for Cynthia to close the door. "I'm freezing enough as it is."

The conversation that follows is awkward to say the least. Multiple rounds of apologies are uttered before I get the chance to explain the whole Fitz thing to Agatha. The reason behind the theft doesn't excuse it, but it certainly paints the act in a different light. Agatha even offers to help put a curse on the man.

Skia points out that's likely unnecessary given how terrified we made him, but I tuck away a mental note to start working on more offensive magic for just such a situation.

We settle in at the store. I plop onto one of the cushy chairs and am draped in a blanket. Missy hops up as well, curling onto my lap. Exhaustion pulls at my eyelids.

Ags gets Cynthia comfortable within a few minutes—as I knew she would. Someone able to pry me out of the introverted shell of a person I was a few years ago is capable of making friends with anyone.

Skia fills in Ags on the level of magic I accomplished, with Cynthia adding in some of the important bits. Like the immediate vomiting afterwards.

Ags brings water to my side, pushing the glass into my hands and urging me to drink every few minutes. When I've drained it, she takes it and tells me to go to sleep.

I'd like to argue. I'm the one who brought Cynthia in. I should be the one to give her the rundown on all things Nona and magic and the farm. But even as I start to protest that I don't need to rest, Missy purrs, and the vibration and the steady rise and fall of her chest lull me to sleep.

· · · ● · ● · ● · · ·

A week later finds all of us, once again, at Nona's. This time with a few extra friends.

Missy skirts through the snow, her dark form standing out amidst the glittering white drifts. Two smaller cats follow her, the little bells around their necks ringing like Christmas bells. They've all been warned, by Cynthia, to stay away from the target practice side of the yard. A fourth figure waits in the shade of the decorated evergreen, red eyes watching the sky for the moment a cloud gives them shade-cover to dart out as well.

The mid-afternoon sun warms the air just enough for a short round of practice spellcasting outside. Nona guides Cynthia's hands, helping her form the right movements with her fingers.

The young woman has acclimated surprisingly fast. Her joy at finding other people able to do magic was amplified by Nona's immediate offer to have her (and the cats, of course) stay on the farm.

Liz takes aim at her target and slams a chunk of rock into the center. A second later she furrows her brow and a cluster of white flowers bloom from the stone.

Cynthia's soft intake of air is drowned out by Ags's loud applause. She and Kate come down the steps of the house, a tray of mugs delicately balanced in Kate's hands.

My eyes go wide. I join them at the base of the steps, my gaze fixed on the mushroom mug Nona fixed with magic after our last visit. I squint up at Kate.

She laughs, the sound loud and free in the open space around us. "Hot chocolate, Demi. With six marshmallows. And it's not too hot."

My fingers close around the mug, and I bring it to my lips. The sweet taste of chocolate coats my tongue.

"Thank you," I say with a sigh. "It's perfect."

We watch Cynthia take a turn. Nona stays by her side, murmuring instructions and guiding her hands to the correct motions. After a minute or two, Cynthia inhales a deep breath, twists her hands in a boxy pattern, and shoots a bolt of what looks like lightning at the target.

It dings off the side of the hay bale, leaving an acrid-smelling scorch mark. But we all burst into applause and cheers anyway.

Cynthia turns, her cheeks flushed. She gives me a wide grin.

I raise my mug in a cheers and take another long sip.

Kate puts a hand on my shoulder. "You doing okay? Recovered?"

I nod truthfully. It took longer than I'd hoped to get myself feeling normal again after finally accomplishing a big moment of magic. The pounding headache for three days reinforced the fact that someone like me needs a focus to help channel.

As though she's reading my mind, Ags appears at my shoulder with a wide grin. "You ready to give it a go?"

I look at her, down at the hot chocolate, then up at her again. I take another sip, the warmth seeping down my chest and settling in my belly. I set the mug down on the steps. "Yeah. Let's see what this thing can do."

"It's not the focus doing it, Demi," Nona calls.

"Her hearing is insane," I mutter.

Kate nods, chuckling. "She's right though. It'll be coming from you."

"I know."

Beside me, Ags reaches into her pocket and pulls out a green velvet bag. Knowing me as well as she does, she refused to hand it over until I'd fully recovered. A smart move, as I probably would've immediately tried to test it out.

I hold out my hands, and from the pouch comes a large silver coin. Not silver, I realize as it lands heavy in my palm. Something denser. But the color of tarnished silver, with some kind of identical symbol pressed on either side. It's a little larger than a half-dollar, and something about the size feels right.

I roll it over in my hands, enjoying the heft of it, and the slightly electric buzz that I recognize as raw magic.

I frown up at Ags. "Does it have magic in it?"

"Nope." She shakes her head.

"I feel..."

"That's yours, Demi," Nona says. She's crossed to us and now puts a hand on my shoulder. "It's already amplifying what you can do."

"Is this..." I look around at her and the others as they form a semi-circle around me. "Is this what you feel all the time?"

Liz holds up her hands. "Mine feels like my hands are in the dirt. Searching for each rock and pebble. Every one I find is a burst of magic."

"Mine is like that, too," Kate says. "Not dirt, but like I can find pockets of magic in the air or something."

Cynthia meets my gaze from the edge of the group, her eyes wide with fresh excitement.

Ags and Nona exchange a glance. Nona takes my arm at the elbow and steers me towards the targets.

"*You've got this, Demi!*" Skia calls as they zip across the snow after the cats. The clouds block the sun, gray taking over the pale blue sky. Skia catches up with Princess, and the pair go tumbling into the white powder.

I laugh, pressing the coin between my fingers.

After this, we'll go inside and start prepping for dinner. Skia will help me make banana bread (they found a recipe in one of Nona's old cookbooks and have been begging to help in the kitchen). We will decorate even more for the solstice tomorrow night. We will study magic from the thick tomes Agatha has been collecting. We will laugh and talk and share ideas for new spells.

I look up at the big farmhouse with its rows of windows and many floors. There are plenty of empty rooms. Plenty of space for new witches to learn how to use their magic.

The smile on my face grows as imaginings of the future pass through my mind.

I put them aside, focusing on the present. On the coin in my hand, and the target down the way, and the family around me cheering me on.

I face the target, press my hands together, and let the magic flow.

Thank you to everyone who continues to read these little stories. I hope they bring you as much joy as they bring me.

The adventures will continue soon.

9 781960 659323